CALUMET CITY PUBLIC

3 1613 00358 2692

S0-AFP-182

PHILOSOPHERS OF
THE ENLIGHTENMENT™

THOMAS HOBBES

An English Philosopher in the Age of Reason

B
HOB

PHILOSOPHERS OF
THE ENLIGHTENMENT™

THOMAS HOBBES An English
Philosopher in
the Age of Reason

Aaron Rosenberg

rosen
central™

The Rosen Publishing Group, Inc., New York

CALUMET CITY PUBLIC LIBRARY

For all those who seek knowledge and truth, even at personal risk

Published in 2006 by The Rosen Publishing Group, Inc.
29 East 21st Street, New York, NY 10010

Copyright © 2006 by The Rosen Publishing Group, Inc.

First Edition

All rights reserved. No part of this book may be reproduced in any form without permission in writing from the publisher, except by a reviewer.

Library of Congress Cataloging-in-Publication Data

Rosenberg, Aaron.
Thomas Hobbes: an English philosopher in the age of reason/
Aaron Rosenberg.—1st ed.
    p. cm.—(Philosophers of the Enlightenment)
Includes bibliographical references (p.).
ISBN 1-4042-0419-9 (library binding)
1. Hobbes, Thomas, 1588–1679—Juvenile literature.
I. Title. II. Series.
B1247.R67 2006
192—dc22

                                                    2004028655

Manufactured in Malaysia

On the cover: Background: View of London along the Thames River from 1616. Inset: A seventeenth-century portrait of Hobbes by Isaac Fuller.

CONTENTS

This is a map of Europe showing important cities during the period of history known as the Enlightenment. The English philosopher Thomas Hobbes spent many years of his adult life in Paris and London, the two cities most often associated with the Enlightenment.

INTRODUCTION

It's sometimes hard to say what you really think, particularly about other people. Too often, we hide our true thoughts and feelings because we don't want to upset someone. Or we lie because we are afraid of what may happen if we tell the truth. This is especially true when dealing with authority figures in our lives—such as parents or teachers.

Some people, however, always say what they think. They don't worry about the consequences. Thomas Hobbes was like that. He spent large portions of his life running from the monarchy, from the church, and from other powerful men and women. Why? Because he had the courage to speak his mind. He spoke his mind even when those thoughts ran against popular belief or might upset powerful people.

Thomas Hobbes (1588–1679) is regarded as one of England's finest philosophers. He is seen here in a portrait from the seventeenth century by Englishman Isaac Fuller. Hobbes is best known for his book *Leviathan*, which introduced a number of new ideas about the role of government. The book caused a great deal of controversy at the time it was published, but Hobbes felt strongly about his ideas and never wavered in defending them.

Thomas Hobbes lived during the sixteenth and seventeenth centuries. He was a brilliant man and is considered one of the first modern scholars. He read literature, wrote poetry, and translated several classic works from other languages. He was also a mathematician, and at times he was considered a mathematical genius.

Above all, Hobbes is remembered as one of history's greatest philosophers. He is especially well known for his political philosophy. During Hobbes's life, the church still held power over most nations and their rulers. People were encouraged to believe that they should answer to the church on all matters. Hobbes refused to accept that. He felt that the church should only control religious activities and nothing else. The church was not happy about his resistance, and made Hobbes's life very difficult.

While Hobbes challenged the church, people around him were rebelling against the king, trying to win freedom. Hobbes rejected them as well. He felt that the king was the ultimate authority in England and that everyone should obey him completely. To Hobbes, going against the king meant going against the entire English society. This earned Hobbes many enemies, but he spoke out anyway. He wasn't trying to win points with the king, either. Hobbes genuinely believed that people were better off when they had a ruler to watch over them and handle most of their problems.

Although he lived through several major conflicts, Hobbes's principal goal was always one of peace. He hoped to find a way to allow everyone to live together without conflict, violence, and war. Even though many of his ideas now seem outdated, Thomas Hobbes was a revolutionary thinker. His ideas and treatises paved the way for many of our modern ideas about the world and our place within it.

ENGLAND IN THE SIXTEENTH CENTURY

CHAPTER 1

2
3
4
5
6

When studying someone from history, it is important to consider the world around him or her. What was happening in the world at that time influenced his or her thoughts and actions. For Hobbes, that influential world begins with England in the sixteenth century.

The first half of the sixteenth century was a time of turmoil in England. Martin Luther had sparked the Protestant Reformation, and his ideas were spreading to England. The Protestants believed that everyone should be offered equal access to God and have equal opportunity for salvation. They felt that the Catholic Church gave too much power to the priests and the nobles. Many people were drawn to these ideas and converted to the new Protestant faith.

HENRY VIII

In 1529, the king of England, Henry VIII, broke away from the Catholic Church. This was shocking because England and its leaders had been loyal to the church and the pope for hundreds of years. Henry VIII created a new church called the Church of England. He did this because he wanted to divorce his wife, Catherine, and marry another woman. However, the pope would not allow it. Henry got around this by declaring that he was replacing the pope as England's spiritual leader. By doing so he was able to give himself permission to divorce. He married Anne Boleyn, only to execute her in 1536 so that he could marry his third wife, Jane Seymour. By the time Henry VIII died in 1547, he had executed many more people, often for religious reasons.

Henry VIII was succeeded by his only son, Edward VI. Edward took religion seriously and tried further to establish England as a Protestant nation. However, some people resisted these changes. They had been Catholic for generations and wanted to stay that way. During Edward's short reign, Catholics and Protestants in England challenged each other for power.

Edward was in poor health and died in 1553. His eldest sister, Mary, became queen after he died. Mary

Anne Boleyn (1507–1536) married King Henry VIII of England in 1533. Their marriage was short and ended tragically after Henry had his wife arrested and charged with adultery. Many historians believe that Anne was innocent of these charges, and that Henry had turned on her because she failed to give birth to a male heir to the throne. In the painting above, Anne is seen in prison shortly after her arrest. She was beheaded on May 19, 1536. Less than two weeks later, Henry married his third wife, Jane Seymour.

was a devout Catholic and wanted to make England Catholic again. To reach this goal, she married the son of the king of Spain, the most powerful Catholic nation in Europe at the time. She had many Protestants executed. She became known as Bloody Mary and was disliked and feared by many people. Like her brother, her reign was short. In 1558, she died and was succeeded by her half sister, Elizabeth, who became Elizabeth I.

GOOD QUEEN BESS

The second half of the century was much calmer. Elizabeth I, known as Good Queen Bess, was a Protestant but allowed other people to practice the religion of their choice. She also supported England's growing middle class and encouraged new businesses and industries. The merchants became stronger and wealthier, and the nation prospered. England's fleet expanded, and its ships sailed all over the world, trading with people in Russia, Canada, and India. The first attempt was made to settle an English colony in North America. Spain had controlled the seas for decades, but now English ships threatened to take control of the Atlantic Ocean.

While the country prospered, the English government began to change. Parliament had always been an advisory board for the throne, and it was filled with nobles and wealthy men who offered suggestions but had no real political power. However, by the end of the century, Elizabeth was having trouble keeping Parliament under control. The MPs (members of Parliament) wanted more say in the government, and they had enough influence to disrupt the kingdom until they got their way. Part of the problem was that Parliament controlled much of the nation's wealth. The queen had to ask Parliament for money whenever she needed some. This meant that the MPs could demand things from her in return.

The other problem was that in 1564, a new religious group had appeared in England. This was the Calvinists, followers of John Calvin, who in England were known as the Puritans. The Puritans did not like either the Church of England or the Catholic Church. They believed that religion needed to be simpler and purified of its excess. Many of the MPs at the end of the century were Puritans. They pushed Elizabeth to give Parliament more power and also to alter the church her father had created.

THE ARMADA

While the Parliament and the queen clashed, there were also threats from outside of the country. In

ROMPTE   ET SINCER

This portrait of John Calvin (1509–1564) was made in the sixteenth century. Calvin is the founder of a religion known as Calvinism. Calvin was born in France and later moved to Switzerland, where he became one of the leading scholars of the Protestant Reformation. The beliefs of Calvinism became the foundation for many similar religions throughout Europe, such as Puritanism in England. During Hobbes's time, the Puritans would become a highly influential group in English society.

1588, the year Hobbes was born, Spain sent its armada to attack England. The attack failed, but many people had been terrified by the sudden threat. They had always known that Spain hated England, but no one expected the Spanish to attack them at home. Many English men and women focused their anger toward their own queen. Elizabeth was getting older and losing control of Parliament and the nobles. Many people felt that she was supposed to protect them from all threats. But if Spain felt strong enough to invade, then clearly she was not doing her job.

PARLIAMENT CHALLENGES THE CROWN

Before the Protestant Reformation, the people had always trusted the king. They believed that he had been chosen by God to rule them. But when Henry VIII broke away from the pope, he shook everyone's faith. Ever since then, people had begun to doubt the king's—and later the queen's—right to rule. During Henry's reign, it was considered treason to argue with the Crown's decisions. Anyone who did so risked a death sentence. But under Elizabeth's reign, people were allowed to discuss and debate more freely. This was especially true with Parliament, which began to resist the queen's decisions without

PLAGUE AND FIRE

Two major events during the mid-seventeenth century shook the foundation of Hobbes's England. The first event was the Great Plague. The second event was the Great Fire of London.

The plague was also known as the black death. It had appeared in London several times, but the worst was the Great Plague outbreak in late 1664. Rats brought the plague into London. Fleas fed on the rats, then on humans, thus passing the

This illustration appeared with a prayer that was intended to protect people from the Great Plague. An estimated 75,000 residents of London were killed by the plague over a two-year period beginning in 1664.

disease to humans through their blood. The plague was incredibly contagious and almost always lethal. It started as little more than a bad cold, but then led to fever, black swellings, and death. At the height of the outbreak, 6,000 people died in a single week. The disease was especially deadly because people did not know how to treat or prevent it. Whenever someone was discovered to have the plague, they were locked in their house to avoid spreading the disease. However, the rest of their family was also locked in and almost always caught the plague soon after.

For two full years, the outbreak ravaged England and spread throughout Europe. Finally, in 1666, the number of plague victims began to drop. By then, it had decimated London and many other major European cities. Hundreds of thousands of people had been killed.

Some people believe that the plague left London because the Great Fire burned it out. This is probably just a coincidence, however. The fire began in a bakery on Pudding Lane, near London Bridge, on September 2, 1666. Most of the buildings in that area were made of wood, and the fire quickly spread. More than 13,000 houses and 87 churches were destroyed by the fire. In two short years, London had lost a large portion of its population, homes, and workplaces.

any negative consequences. Soon, members of Parliament were openly defying her.

At the same time, the nation was torn between Roman Catholicism and the various Protestant faiths, including Lutheranism, Anglicanism, and Puritanism. Leaders in each of these Christian sects wanted control over the nation and often resorted to violence to remove their opponents. By the start of the seventeenth century, England was filled with anger, doubt, and hatred. Everyone wanted control. The new king, James I, was desperately trying to hold all the pieces together.

HOBBES IN ENGLISH SOCIETY

Unfortunately, as he grew older, Hobbes found himself caught at the center of the struggle. After college, Hobbes became a tutor for a wealthy noble family. This association with the upper crust of English society would make him a target. For example, Hobbes was good friends with the man who became King Charles II. Anyone who knew that might try to hurt the king by attacking his friend. Because of this threat, Hobbes often fled to Paris for long periods of time.

Moving in court society allowed Hobbes to watch the king and his courtiers control the English

The children of Charles I of England are pictured in this painting from the seventeenth century. They are, from left to right, Charles, the prince of Wales; James, the Duke of York; and Princess Mary. About ten years after this painting was made, Thomas Hobbes became the tutor of the prince of Wales, the future king of England.

government. Many people were frightened by what the king could do to them. Hobbes was both frightened and impressed, because now he could see how government worked. From these observations, Hobbes learned a lot about what it meant to be king. He learned how much pressure the king was under and how the nation's survival truly depended upon the strength of its ruler.

Even though he saw firsthand how human and how fallible the king was, Hobbes still admired him and wanted him to run the country with a firm hand. Others felt this indicated Hobbes's love of monarchy and tyranny. They considered him a traitor to the common man. Yet, later in his life, all of his writings were concerned with improving the life of the common man. Hobbes's writings encouraged his fellow citizens to support the king, but that was because Hobbes felt the nation needed a single strong leader to survive. His greatest concern was that England would fall into chaos without a proper ruler.

THE PHILOSOPHER EMERGES

CHAPTER 2

Thomas Hobbes was born in Malmesbury, England, on April 5, 1588. According to legend, his mother was so frightened about the invasion of the Spanish armada that she went into labor early. He happened to be born on Good Friday, a Christian holy day. To his family, this probably was a sign that God had a special plan for young Thomas.

Thomas was the second son of Thomas Hobbes, the vicar of the Westport Church. The family lived in a two-story stone house, right across from the church itself. Thomas had a brother, Edmund, who was two years older, and a younger sister whose name is not known.

When Thomas was seven years old, his father got into an argument

Seen above is the abbey in Malmesbury, the town where Hobbes was born. Malmesbury is in southwest England in the county of Wiltshire. The abbey was finished in 1180 and contained one of the largest libraries in Europe. In 1539, Henry VIII seized the abbey from the Catholic Church and sold it to a wealthy merchant. This painting was made in the nineteenth century by the English artist J. M. W. Turner.

with another vicar. The argument occurred on the doorstep of the church. The argument got out of hand, and the two men exchanged blows. This was a serious crime, and the elder Hobbes fled to avoid punishment. He never returned, leaving his brother to raise the children in his place.

In a way, this was a blessing for Thomas. His uncle, Francis Hobbes, was a wealthy merchant with no children of his own. He took a great interest in his niece and nephews and supported them generously. His wealth allowed him to pay for their education.

Schooling was expensive at the time, and without his uncle's support Thomas would never have gone beyond elementary education.

EARLY EDUCATION

At four years old, Thomas began his studies at the school in Westport Church. He proved to be a bright pupil. By age eight he could read well and handle addition and subtraction up to four digits. That was as far as the church could teach him, so Thomas moved on to a different school. This larger school was in Malmesbury and was run by Mr. Evans, the town minister. But Thomas soon learned everything the minister could teach him and had to find another teacher.

This time he wound up with Robert Latimer. Latimer was only nineteen or twenty himself and had recently finished college. He had settled in the Malmesbury area and offered private tutoring. Thomas was one of only three or four students and was apparently Latimer's favorite. This was partially because he was a pleasant boy and a good conversationalist, but also because he was a brilliant student. Thomas was also very focused. When given a lesson, he would set everything else aside until he had learned the lesson by heart. By the time he was

This map of England was made in 1605, when Hobbes was seventeen years old. England's unique location has had a great impact on its history. Because it is an island, water has provided a natural barrier from attacks by land forces. During Hobbes's time, threats to the country would arrive via fleets of battleships, such as the attack of the Spanish armada in 1588.

fourteen, Thomas had become an excellent scholar of Greek and Latin. Before leaving Mr. Latimer's care, Thomas translated Euripedes's play *Medea* from the original Greek into Latin. He presented the translation to his teacher as a parting gift.

ADVANCED SCHOOLING

In 1603, at the age of fourteen, Thomas Hobbes had learned everything Robert Latimer felt qualified to teach him. But still he craved more. He turned to his Uncle Francis for money and applied to the University of Oxford, one of the most prestigious colleges in England. Hobbes was accepted into Magdalen Hall and studied there for the next five years. Hobbes enjoyed his time at Oxford, but was not thrilled with all of his studies. The school was teaching ancient logic at the time, which Hobbes didn't find very interesting. He frequently skipped logic lectures to spend time reading or studying maps. Hobbes was pleased to learn more

This is a contemporary photograph of Magdalen Hall, a famous landmark at the University of Oxford in England. Hobbes studied at Magdalen Hall from 1603 to 1608. Hobbes was a good student and used the knowledge he gained at Oxford to become the tutor of some of the most influential figures in seventeenth-century England.

Greek and Latin, however, and quickly impressed all of his professors with his skill.

LIFE AS A TUTOR

In 1608, Hobbes graduated from Oxford. The principal of Magdalen Hall, Sir James Hussey, thought highly of Hobbes. He recommended Hobbes for a position as a private tutor.

The Cavendish family hired him to tutor their son, William. The elder William Cavendish was the

Baron of Hardwick and later the Earl of Devonshire. His son and heir was only a few years younger than Hobbes, but the baron felt that his son would learn more from a tutor his own age than from an older and more intimidating tutor.

In many ways, Hobbes was more of a companion than a tutor to William. He and William became life-long friends. They spent most of their time riding, hunting, and hawking. This was Hobbes's first real taste of how the wealthy lived their lives. From the Cavendish family and their friends, he learned a great deal about the way the nation worked and what the people in power thought and did from day to day.

A TOUR OF EUROPE

The wealthy families of England often sent their children on tours of Europe after their formal schooling was finished. In 1610, Hobbes accompanied William on such a trip. They visited France, Germany, and Italy. Hobbes was able to learn both French and Italian during the trip. Hobbes also learned about European scientific methods and discovered that he preferred them to the philosophy he had learned at Oxford.

After Hobbes returned to England, he began studying Greek and Latin again. He had forgotten much of his Latin over the past few years, but he picked it up again very quickly. He was able to improve his skill by doing translations. William Cavendish did not really need a tutor anymore, so Hobbes became his secretary instead. This job required very little, leaving Hobbes with ample time for his own studies. He began by reading romances and plays. After two years, he decided that these were a waste of his time. He switched to weightier topics, including Thucydides's *History of the Peloponnesian Wars*. He spent the next fifteen years working on an English translation of that great work.

LESSONS FROM A GREEK HISTORIAN

In *History of the Peloponnesian Wars*, Thucydides writes about how understanding the past was necessary in order to behave correctly in the present. Hobbes felt that this was an important lesson, especially with all the turmoil in English politics. He also felt that people needed to be reminded that the ancient Greeks had considered democracy an inferior form of government. In their eyes, a group of people contained too many different personalities and conflicting goals to make unified and smart decisions.

Hobbes, like many scholars of his time, enjoyed studying the history of ancient Greece. This stone carving was created in Greece in the sixth century BC and depicts two warriors and the god Hera, who was believed to accompany soldiers into battle.

LOSS OF A FRIEND

In 1626, William's father died and William became the second Earl of Devonshire. Unfortunately, William himself died two years later, succumbing to the plague in June 1628. Hobbes lost his closest friend. Then, soon after William's death, his widow informed Hobbes that the family no longer required his services. This must have disappointed Hobbes immensely, but it also motivated him to work even harder on his studies. In these sad times, he found inspiration in the great books of history and philosophy.

KING JAMES I

Queen Elizabeth I died in 1603. She had never married and had no heirs, so the crown went to her distant cousin, James VI of Scotland. He became James I of England.

For many, this was not a fair trade. They lost Elizabeth, a lovely, graceful woman renowned for

her wisdom and control. And in her place they got James, a small, plump man with poor social graces and frequent bouts of illness.

James was well educated, however, and an expert on the Bible. He was also an experienced ruler, since he was already the king of Scotland.

James I (1566–1625) poses in this portrait from the early seventeenth century. In addition to being the king of England, James was also the king of Scotland. James was not well-liked by his subjects. His policies set the foundation for the English Civil War.

Unfortunately, some of James's ideas did not go over well at the time. His belief in the divine right of kings was especially a problem. This was an old idea that kings were appointed directly by God and thus represented God on Earth. Questioning or opposing the king meant opposing God, and in the seventeenth century this was unthinkable. This idea had been popular during the Middle Ages, but during the past century it had fallen out of favor. This was particularly true during Elizabeth's reign. Because of this, James inherited a Parliament of wealthy men who believed that the king was just another man. Parliament believed that they had as much right as the king did to govern the nation.

THE MATHEMATICIAN

It didn't take Hobbes long to find more work. He was soon employed to tutor the son of Sir Gervase Clifton of Nottinghamshire. It was during this period that Hobbes finally published his translation of Thucydides. However, that would be the last of his translations for a while. He had found a new interest that distracted him from his translation work. In 1628, at the age of forty, Thomas Hobbes discovered mathematics.

According to close friend and later biographer James Aubrey, Hobbes was visiting a friend and found himself waiting in the other man's library. He noticed a book sitting open upon the desk and paused to examine it. The book was Euclid's *Elements*, a classic mathematics text. Hobbes opened to a page detailing Euclid's forty-seventh proposition. As Aubrey puts it: "He read the proposition. 'By God,' said he, 'this is impossible!' So he reads the demonstration of it, which referred him back to such a proof; which referred him back to another, which he also read . . . at last he was demonstratively convinced of that truth. This made him in love with geometry."

Euclid convinced Hobbes that the only way to demonstrate anything was through deductive reasoning. He began to study and consider such logic systems, and a few years later he published his second work, *A Short Treatise on First Principles*.

This book discusses physical sensation in terms of mathematics. Hobbes's ideas are based on the belief that people are essentially complex machines. Physical sensation is simply a series of processes within the body and mind, activated by pressure against the body. The processes are all logical, which means they can be explained using mathematical equations. Hobbes believed that everything, even thoughts and emotions, could be understood by math.

PARIS

Working for Sir Clifton took Hobbes to Paris in 1629. This was his second trip to the European continent. Again, he enjoyed himself immensely. Sir Clifton and Hobbes stayed in Paris for the next two years. In between tutoring sessions, Hobbes spent his time meeting French mathematicians and philosophers and refining his own theories. He hoped to use mathematics, and particularly logical reasoning, to find solutions to societal problems he saw in English society. This would become a trait of Hobbes's work. He wanted to look at problems rationally instead of emotionally. By reducing the problems to mathematical puzzles, he could look at them more objectively. Throughout his stay in Paris, Hobbes focused on obtaining the knowledge and skills to help him do this.

THE PHILOSOPHER

In 1631, William Cavendish's widow asked Hobbes to come back to England and tutor her son. Hobbes happily complied. Hobbes tutored the third Earl of Devonshire from 1631 to 1642. During this period, he took his third trip to continental Europe, staying there with the young earl from 1634 to 1637. During

This painting shows Paris in the early seventeenth century. Featured in the painting is the Seine River, an important waterway for transportation and commerce. Paris at the time was one of the leading cultural centers in Europe. During his time in Paris, Hobbes met some of the most brilliant minds of the day. These people and the ideas they shared with him would help shape the way Hobbes saw the world.

this trip, Hobbes met the mathematician-philosophers Galileo Galilei, Marin Mersenne, René Descartes, Pierre Gassendi, and Gilles de Roberval. These five great men heavily influenced his own thinking. After meeting them, Hobbes began modifying his philosophy to encompass new ideas.

He was particularly taken with Galileo's work. Galileo claimed that the natural state of an object was in motion, not at rest as many people believed. That meant that things were always moving unless

CHARLES I AND PARLIAMENT

James I died in 1625 and was succeeded by his son, Charles I. Charles believed in the divine right of kings, just as his father had. But Parliament had become even more of a threat to the king's power over the years. MPs argued with the king constantly. They were demanding changes in the Church of England. They also suspected that Charles was secretly supporting the Catholics, who were still trying to regain control over the nation.

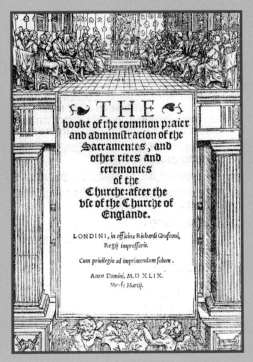

In 1629, Charles tried to tax the English people and Parliament tried to stop him. Outraged, Charles dissolved Parliament. For the next eleven years—known by many as the Eleven Years'

A dispute between King Charles I and church officials in Scotland over use of the Book of Common Prayer *(pictured above) would lead to a bloody civil war between Parliament and the English crown.*

Tyranny—he ruled without any help from Parliament. Unfortunately Charles took advantage of this independence to revive old taxes, which angered people further.

In 1637, Charles tried forcing Scotland to use the Church of England prayer book. The Puritan Scots refused. In response, Charles raised an army to attack them. Soon, he learned he needed more money to pay the troops and was forced to recall Parliament. Parliament reconvened in November 1640. It refused to help Charles unless he agreed to certain conditions. The first was that Parliament could never again be dissolved. The second was that only Parliament had the right to raise taxes. The king was desperate and agreed. Parliament immediately had the archbishop, William Laud, imprisoned, and Charles's chief minister, Thomas Wentworth, executed. The following year, Parliament issued what it called the Grand Remonstrance, a list of demands that would significantly increase its power and reduce the role of the king.

By 1642, Charles had had enough. He took 400 soldiers and set out to arrest the five most difficult MPs. But they escaped his grasp and took control of the army. Charles refused to surrender, however, and put together his own army. Now the nation had two armies: the Royalists and the Parliamentarians.

something stopped them. Hobbes not only agreed with this idea, but he felt that it could be used to explain human behavior as well. Hobbes's theory was that people were always in motion, heading toward their own goals. If no one stopped them or got in their way, they would ultimately reach their goals.

SHARING IDEAS

In Paris, Hobbes became close to a group of Mersenne's friends. This group liked to gather and discuss politics and other important topics. Hobbes became a valuable member of the group, known for his skill in debate. It was during this period, in 1637, that Hobbes began to refer to himself as a philosopher. He also began planning an ambitious book about his social theories. He planned to write the book in three parts. In the first, he would talk about general laws of motion. In the second part, he would discuss how people are bodies in motion because they are always motivated by something and because they can be affected by external motion. In the third and final section, he would deal with how the motions and motivations of people created politics and society.

LIFE ON THE RUN

Hobbes came back home in 1637 to find England divided and discontent. The king had broken up Parliament and raised taxes. These decisions angered many people. During these tense times, Hobbes spent his time writing his next work, *Elements of Law*, *Natural and Politic*, which was released privately in 1640. It focuses upon how men relate to one another in society and the rules that must be followed for a society to function properly.

A MARKED MAN

A few years later, Hobbes left England again, but this time it was for a less pleasant reason. Parliament had reconvened and was actively trying to depose the king. Hobbes was solidly Royalist and had made this clear in his writing. This made him a target for Parliament and its allies. To avoid them, Hobbes thought it safest to flee the country. He returned to Paris and his friend Mersenne's circle of scholars. While in Paris, Hobbes published a set of objections to his friend Descartes' *Meditations on First Philosophy*. A year later, Descartes would respond to these objections. Unfortunately, their remarks back and forth grew more bitter

This painting of René Descartes (1596–1650) was made by Sebastian Bourdon in the seventeenth century. Descartes remains one of the most influential philosophers and mathematicians in history. He is especially well known for his contributions to the study of geometry.

each time. Within a few years, the two stopped corresponding altogether.

While in Paris, Hobbes also wrote *On the Citizen* (often known by its Latin title, *De Cive*), which was the second part of what would ultimately be a trilogy. *On the Citizen* was finished in November 1641. At first, Hobbes only circulated it privately. The book deals with Hobbes's ideas about the relationship between church and state. He allowed it to be

THE FIRST ENGLISH CIVIL WAR

By 1642, Charles I had his army and the members of Parliament had theirs. Neither side was willing to back down. Parliament issued the Nineteen Propositions, which was another set of demands for reform. Charles refused and a civil war began.

Parliament had the early advantage. It controlled London and most of the nation's wealth.

Depicted above is the Battle of Marston Moor in 1644, one of the largest battles of the English Civil War. The battle was a decisive victory for the army of the Parliament.

The king had more men but no money to pay them. Neither side had much experience, since England was used to fighting naval battles and not land battles.

In October 1642, the king's men marched on London. They encountered the parliamentary army at Edgehill and forced them to retreat. Despite this success, the king's men could not overcome the rest of the parliamentary forces or take control of London. The king tried enlisting aid from Ireland, but the few troops who were sent weren't much help. Parliament turned to Scotland. The Scottish troops ended up being instrumental in destroying the king's northern forces.

By 1644, most of the Royalists were convinced that they would lose the battle, so they fled the country. Many of the fleeing Royalists ran to Paris. Hobbes was living there at the time and became reacquainted with many old friends. He decided to reprint *On the Citizen* and distribute it more widely. It found great favor among the Royalists, who completely agreed with his theories.

In June 1645, the two armies met at Naseby, Leicestershire. Oliver Cromwell led the parliamentary army, and this time they soundly defeated the Royalists. By May 1646, Charles was forced to surrender to Parliament.

printed more widely after many of his friends complimented his work. He then published a short treatise on optics (*Tractatus Opticus*). This was included in the collection of scientific tracts published by Mersenne as *Cogitata Physico-Mathematica* (Thoughts in Mathematical Physics).

During these years in Paris, Hobbes became well known as a philosopher. In 1645, he was even chosen by Descartes, Roberval, and others to referee a debate between two prominent philosophers, John Pell and Longomontanus. In 1646, he published *A Minute or First Draught of the Optiques*, which covers his theories on optical images and the relation between vision, image, and reality.

POLITICAL DANGERS

Hobbes enjoyed his time in Europe, but he still longed for home. He kept an eye on the situation in England, waiting for the fighting to end and his political enemies to forget him. Hobbes spent most of his time in Paris, although he did visit Italy and a few other nations. He often met with his friends to debate science and philosophy. But Hobbes also worked during this period. From 1646 to 1648, he tutored King Charles's son (also named Charles) in mathematics. The two got along quite well. However,

CHARLES I AND CROMWELL

After his defeat at Naseby, Charles I went to the Scots for help. They promptly handed him over to Parliament. The MPs were ready to give him back the throne, provided his powers were severely limited. Oliver Cromwell, a general and one of the leaders of the parliamentary army, supported this proposal. Charles pretended to agree but instead planned a second attack.

The second war was mainly a series of small uprisings and did not last long. The Royalists were defeated again, and the king was arrested again. Charles I was found guilty of treason and was sentenced to death. The sentence was carried out on January 30, 1649.

Oliver Cromwell (1599–1658) appears in his battle gear in this painting from the mid-seventeenth century. Cromwell was an intensely religious man and recruited soldiers for his army who held similar beliefs.

Afterward, Cromwell reduced Parliament to 140 handpicked men.

Within months it became clear that the new Parliament was not strong enough to run the country effectively. In 1653, Cromwell took control more directly. He marched into Westminster with the army behind him, dissolved Parliament, and named himself lord protector of England.

Oliver Cromwell ruled England as a military dictator from 1649 to 1653. He crushed rebellions in Ireland, blocked Charles II's attempts to invade from Scotland, and divided the nation into military districts. Each of these districts was controlled by a military commander who answered directly to Cromwell.

It was a strange period in England. There was no king, no Parliament, no lords, and no church. Theaters and other amusements were destroyed, and religious festivals were banned. Although Cromwell's government improved England in some ways, it was overly restrictive and very expensive, which made it very unpopular.

When Cromwell died in 1658, his son Richard became lord protector. Richard lacked his father's strength and did not have the army's support. The country called for the return of the king. Charles II was invited back from Holland and returned triumphantly in May 1660.

their sessions abruptly ended when Charles was sent to Holland so he could be kept safe from his father's enemies. Finally, in 1651, Hobbes felt the situation in England had cooled down enough and he returned home.

HOBBES'S BOOKS REAPPEAR

In 1647, Hobbes expanded and republished *On the Citizen*. In 1650, *Elements of Law, Natural and Politic* was published again as well, but this new edition appeared without his permission.

The unauthorized *Elements of Law* appeared in two parts. The first was called *Human Nature* (Humane Nature) and the second was *Of the Body Politic* (De Corpore Politico). The books were based upon his earlier manuscripts. As a result, they were rougher than his other books and had several errors.

LEVIATHAN

In 1647, Hobbes became seriously ill. It is not clear what this illness was, but it disabled him for six full months. During those months, Hobbes was unable to write, but he had plenty of time to think. His thoughts were focused on his next project. This would be his greatest work yet.

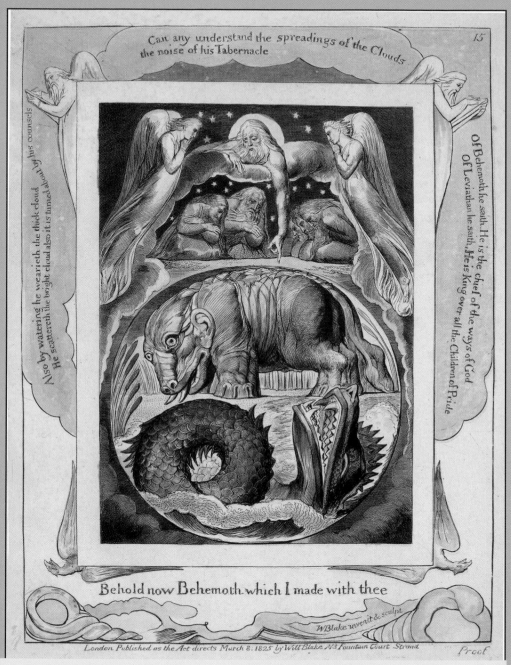

The Behemoth *(top creature in inset)* and the Leviathan *(bottom creature in inset)* are depicted in this eighteenth-century engraving by English artist William Blake. Both creatures are formidable beasts that appear in the Old Testament and in early Mesopotamian myths. In the Bible, the leviathan is portrayed as a sea monster, while the behemoth is an enormous land-dwelling creature. In Hobbes's book *Leviathan*, the creature Leviathan, because of its great strength and power, served as a symbol of government.

In 1651, Hobbes finished and published *Leviathan, or the Matter, Form and Power of a Commonwealth, Ecclesiastical and Civil*. The title of the book was a reference to the Bible, in which the Leviathan is a legendary sea monster. *Leviathan* was Hobbes's longest and most complicated work. It talked about government as a monster composed of men but possessing a life of its own.

Although philosophers admired the book a great deal, it angered many politicians and church officials. The Puritans disliked it because they knew that Hobbes was still a Royalist, and they could see that in his writing. At the same time, the Royalists thought that Hobbes was trying to make peace with Cromwell's government, and they hated him for giving in. In reality, Hobbes's beliefs had not changed. He believed that citizens owed their ruler allegiance, but only as long as the ruler could properly protect them. Unfortunately, many of the Royalists felt that the king should be obeyed no matter what happened, simply because he was the king.

In *Leviathan* Hobbes discusses religion as well as politics. Throughout, he attacks the Catholic Church. This didn't matter much in London, but Paris was still staunchly Catholic. Hobbes suddenly found himself less welcome in his home away from home. He

The city of London along the Thames River is seen in this engraving from 1616. During Hobbes's time, London was the cultural and artistic capital of England and the seat of its government. It was also the largest city in England. Hobbes lived in London in the 1650s. During this time, he was able to discuss and debate important issues of the day with many of the finest philosophers in London.

decided that perhaps it was time to go back to England, present himself to the government, and hope for the best.

He returned to England in the winter of 1651, and submitted himself to the council of state. It granted him amnesty, and he was allowed to settle into a small house in London.

NEARING THE END

By 1659, Hobbes was living in a nice home called Little Salisbury House. The following year, his former pupil Charles II became the king of England. One day, Charles was passing through Hobbes's neighborhood just as Hobbes happened to be standing by his front gate. The king stopped and asked Hobbes how he was doing. A week later, he sent for his old tutor again. The two renewed their friendship. Charles granted a generous pension to Hobbes, who was now in his seventies.

Hobbes was still actively working at this time. He wrote a new treatise, *On Laws* (De Legibus), which unfortunately

CHARLES II

Charles II was very different from his father. The new king was tall, dark, cheerful, witty, and full of fun. After years of Puritan rule, the people were delighted with him.

Despite this, the people were not willing to give the king ultimate power again. Charles realized this and let Parliament handle certain

matters. For example, Parliament would be given power to decide how the country's finances should be handled. Parliament was also granted control over all forms of taxation.

The Church of England became the official church again, but many people practiced other religions. Charles was

Hobbes's former student, Charles II (1630–1685), is seen in this painting from the seventeenth century. Charles was nicknamed the "Merry Monarch" because of his charm and easygoing nature.

secretly Catholic and hoped to restore Catholicism as the state religion of England. In 1672, he introduced the Declaration of Indulgences, which granted religious tolerance to everyone, including Catholics. Parliament, which had many Puritan members, refused to pass the declaration. Instead it passed the Test Act, which excluded Roman Catholics from holding any public office. This forced the king's brother, James, the Duke of York and Charles's heir, into exile. With the king's brother out of the picture, Parliament successfully blocked Charles's attempts to return England to Catholic rule.

was never printed. Several of his friends read it, however, and admired it a great deal.

Hobbes spent much of his time at court entertaining the king with conversation. The rest of his day was often spent meditating in his garden. He liked to sit and think during the morning, jotting down notes from time to time. In the afternoon, he would organize his thoughts and work on his writing projects.

HERETICAL VIEWS

Now that Hobbes was close to the king, more and more people heard his name and read his works.

THOMAS HOBBES MALMESBURIENSIS

Compositum jus, fasque, animi, sanctosque recessus.
Mentis, & incoctum generoso pectus honesto.
Hæc cedo, ut admoveam templis, & farre litabo.

from the Original Devonshire House Piccadilly.

Perf. Sat. 2.

The text bordering this engraving identifies the subject as "Thomas Hobbes Malmesburiensis," which is another way of saying "Thomas Hobbes of Malmesbury." This practice of identifying men by the towns in which they were born or grew up was common in England in the seventeenth century.

Many of them hated his ideas, particularly the Puritans and the Catholics. People had also begun to point out the errors in his mathematics. His reputation in that field had changed from a highly respected mathematician to someone who was considered barely capable in the subject.

In 1666, the House of Commons introduced a bill against atheism and heresy. Hobbes and *Leviathan* were targeted particularly, because of the way Hobbes spoke against religion throughout that work. Hobbes was terrified that he might be declared a heretic. He even burned many of his important papers to prevent members of the House of Commons from reading them. He also wrote three short dialogues, which were added as an appendix to the 1668 Latin translation of *Leviathan*. In these dialogues, Hobbes discusses the definition of heresy to prove that he was not guilty of such a crime.

Fortunately, the king stepped in to protect his former tutor. Hobbes was never formally charged with a crime. He did have trouble publishing his work after that, however. The 1668 version of *Leviathan* was published in Amsterdam because Hobbes could not get permission to publish it in England. Still, Hobbes labored on and found ways to get published. He wrote an autobiography in 1672.

This was followed by an English translation of the first four books of Homer's *Odyssey* in 1673, followed by a complete translation of Homer's *Iliad* and the *Odyssey* in 1675. By this time, Hobbes was in his late eighties.

THE END ITSELF

In 1675, Hobbes left London for good. He moved to Derbyshire, where he spent his time with his old friend Cavendish, the third Earl of Devonshire. In October 1679, Thomas Hobbes suffered a fatal stroke. He was ninety-one years old. Amazingly, he had been working on another book shortly before his death. His last words were said to be, "I am about to take my last voyage, a great leap in the dark." Hobbes died on December 4, 1679. He was buried in the churchyard of Ault Hucknall in Derbyshire.

THE BOOKS

1
2
3
5
6

CHAPTER 4

During his day, Hobbes was considered a scientist (especially in the field of optics), a mathematician (especially in geometry), a translator, a tutor, a philosopher, and a debater. But he was best known as a writer, especially for his writings on morality and politics. It is these writings that have earned him a place in history.

ELEMENTS OF LAW

His first philosophical book was *Elements of Law, Natural and Politic*, which he finished in 1640. Hobbes did not have the book published, but instead gave copies to friends and colleagues, including members of Parliament. The book was printed in 1650 without his permission and divided into two volumes: *Human Nature* and *Of the Body Politic*.

Elements of Law grew out of Hobbes's theories about how motion and society are related. He had decided to write a three-part treatise on this topic. The first part would deal with the laws of motion themselves. The second part would single out humanity and explain how people were dominated by their motions and how every action was motivated by some desire. The third section would deal with how human motion produced society and politics.

After Hobbes devised the plan for his treatise, the situation back home in England grew worse, particularly for those still loyal to the king. Because of this, Hobbes decided to reverse the order of the sections, dealing with the more pressing problems first. Hobbes had limited time to write and was only able to include the second and third parts of his plan. This book became *Elements of Law*. The expanded three-part treatise would have to be put off until a later date.

This portrait of Hobbes was made around 1642, shortly after he finished his book *Elements of Law*. This book introduced readers to many of the ground-breaking ideas that would reappear in his books *On the Citizen* and *Leviathan*. Perhaps the most famous of these ideas was the social contract, which described how power should be distributed between individual citizens and the government.

In *Elements of Law*, Hobbes explains how people are ruled by their desires. This does not make people good or bad. It only means that everyone is focused upon his or her own interests. This trait makes cooperation almost impossible in the long term. So, in order for people to live together peacefully, they need someone to tell them what to do. This person is the king. Hobbes believed it is necessary to surrender all authority to this king so that he can govern effectively.

THE SOCIAL CONTRACT

In writing *Elements of Law*, Hobbes created the idea of the social contract. People accept this unwritten contract by taking part in society, he said. Everyone has to accept it and follow its rules for society to work properly.

Hobbes believed social contracts can change with time. A small group of people may form a democratic society and agree to share responsibility and power. But as the group grows larger, it may become necessary for one person to take control. That means everyone else has to accept the leader's authority. Then, the social contract changes, and each person has to either accept the changes or leave the society. In a monarchy like England, the contract states that all power resides in the king. Parliament, by opposing Charles I's orders and trying to limit his authority, was violating that contract and disrupting the society.

THE TRILOGY

As mentioned earlier, Hobbes had intended for many years to write a three-part treatise on his ideas about motion, man, and society. The events in England had caused him to change the order and merge the second and third parts into a single work, *Elements of Law*. But Hobbes still planned to release all three sections as separate books. In 1642, he published *On the Citizen*, a revised and expanded version of *Elements of Law*'s second half. In 1655, he published *On the Body* (De Corpore), and in 1658 he released the third and final section, *On Man* (De Homine).

ON THE CITIZEN

On the Citizen focuses upon the proper organization of people in society. The end of the book concentrates on religion and the proper relation between church and state. This was a very important subject at that time, particularly in England, where the Church of England, the Puritans, and the Catholics were still fighting for control. According to Hobbes, a Christian church and a Christian state should be considered a single unit, which meant that the king was the head of both. That gave the king the right to settle religious disputes, determine the proper forms of worship, and even interpret the Bible. In other words, *On the Citizen* supported the king's role as the head of the Church of England. Some critics believe that although *Leviathan* is better known, *On the Citizen* gives a much more straightforward account of Hobbes's ideas about political systems.

ON THE BODY

In 1655, several years after returning to England for good, Hobbes published the second portion of the trilogy, *On the Body*. In the book, Hobbes writes about the general laws of motion and how they affect every object. The book contains a great deal of math. This is partially because Hobbes felt that math could help us understand the rules of society. He also believed that his mathematical ideas were revolutionary, and in *On the Body* he hoped to change how people study mathematics.

HOBBES'S FAULTY MATH

Hobbes's approach was extremely materialistic and avoided abstract ideas. To Hobbes, math was all about quantity, measurement of three-dimensional bodies, and motion.

Unfortunately, not all of Hobbes's math was correct. Before *On the Body* was finished, several friends pointed out an error in his explanation of how to square a circle. Hobbes renamed the section "From a false hypothesis, a false quadrature," but did not remove it from the book. He added a second explanation, but was not confident in it and named it "an approximate quadrature." Then he attempted a third explanation, but as the book was being printed Hobbes realized that this explanation was also incorrect. It was too late to remove the argument completely. Hobbes quickly added a claim that the argument should not be taken as a literal proof, but only as an example of the problems involved. This earned him scorn from several critics, particularly the prominent mathematician John Wallis. Hobbes replied that Wallis only understood algebra, which would make him unable to understand the geometry on which Hobbes was working.

This portrait of John Wallis (1616–1703) was painted in 1701 by Sir Godfrey Kneller. Wallis was an English mathematician and professor at the University of Oxford. Many considered him to be the most influential English mathematician of his time. He made important contributions to many areas of math, including algebra, geometry, and calculus. For more than twenty years, Wallis and Hobbes were enemies and became involved in a vicious argument over whose mathematical analysis was more accurate.

ON MAN

Three years after publishing *On the Body*, Hobbes published the final section of the trilogy, *On Man*. This book takes the laws of motion Hobbes describes in *On the Body* and applies them to man, specifically thought and appetite. The book was an expansion of the first half of *Elements of Law*. It bridged the gap between *On the Body* and *On the Citizen*. In *On Man*, Hobbes states that people are active forces, constantly in motion, and that their motions could be described and even predicted using geometric principles.

LEVIATHAN

CHAPTER 5

After his illness in 1646, Hobbes began writing *Leviathan, or the Matter, Form and Power of a Commonwealth, Ecclesiastical and Civil.* It took him five years to complete it, but the effort was well worth it. *Leviathan* would become known as Hobbes's masterpiece.

Leviathan is divided into four sections. The first two parts, "Of Man" and "Of Commonwealth," expand upon the ideas Hobbes had already presented in *Elements of Law.* He would later rework these same ideas and present them in *On Man* and a revised *On the Citizen.* The last two sections, "Of a Christian Commonwealth" and "Of the Kingdom of Darkness," are a discussion of scripture and an attack on the people who had challenged Charles I's rights as king. It was these last sections that made Hobbes so unpopular in Paris and forced him to flee back to London.

This is the title page from *Leviathan, or the Matter, Form and Power of a Commonwealth, Ecclesiastical and Civil*. The book, first published in London in 1651, is considered by many to be Hobbes's masterpiece. The towering figure wearing the crown is made out of the bodies of many smaller men. To Hobbes, this figure represented the Leviathan, within whom all the power of the state was contained.

THOUGHTS ON HUMAN NATURE

Some philosophers have claimed that humankind is inherently good, while others believe humankind is inherently evil. Hobbes did not support either view. Instead, he stated that people were naturally selfish and instinctively chose whatever best satisfied their desires. This is because people are driven by their senses. The need to satisfy those senses is greater than any other need. This all fits with Hobbes's belief in the power of motion. For example, hunger is a motion of the body. Eating is simply an attempt to remove that hunger and quiet that motion.

Hobbes's beliefs are pessimistic about human nature. He believed that if left to his or her own devices, each person will be out for himself or herself alone. Using the example of people as objects in motion, he believed people would simply crash into one another because no one would be willing to yield. This would lead to chaos and anarchy in society. Hobbes imagined a world before law, when everyone existed in their natural state, and he concluded that life would be "solitary, poore, nasty, brutish and short." Obviously, this was not acceptable.

Fortunately, Hobbes believed that people had the ability to make rational decisions. At the same time, they were also inherently afraid of death. That meant that most people's sense of survival would overcome their destructive instincts. For example, no one would want violence used against them, and so they all might agree to renounce violence together. That way, everyone could pursue their own interests in peace and safety.

However, Hobbes saw a hole in this theory. If even one person broke that agreement and used violence, everyone else would be forced to defend themselves and this could lead to a larger conflict. And, in a group of people, Hobbes argued, it would be highly unlikely that every single person would never break the contract. Inevitably, the contract would be broken.

ROLE OF THE STATE

To avoid this problem, Hobbes believed that an outside force had to be added. This was the state, or the Leviathan. The type of Leviathan did not matter, as long as everyone agreed to surrender authority to it. The state, in turn, agreed to use that power to maintain peace.

Since the state's power came from the people, there was a built-in protection against abuse of power. If the state failed to serve the people, the people could reclaim their power, strip the state of its might, and create a new and improved state.

MORALITY

One important aspect of Hobbes's theories, as detailed in *Leviathan*, is his view of morality. Many philosophers believe that certain moral values are part of nature and that people instinctively obey them. Hobbes disagreed. He felt that morals, justice, liberty, and other concepts were mere social constructs. People agreed to certain ideals and gave the state the power to enforce them, or the state created the ideals and the people approved them. But either way, these ideals had no value outside of society. Part of his proof was that different societies have different definitions of justice, morality, and liberty. These ideals are not fixed, but evolve to suit the setting and circumstances.

THE IMPORTANCE OF LAWS

In *Leviathan*, Hobbes also discusses laws and why they are important. He points out that laws only have meaning when the lawgivers have the authority to support them. No matter how right it sounded, a "law" proposed by someone other than the state was not really a law because it had no power behind it. At the same time, any law passed by the state was considered just, because justice was merely a matter of obeying the rules of that state. Thus, it was impossible to have an unjust law. If the law existed, it must be part of the state and that made it just. In many ways, this matched James I's and Charles I's belief in the divine right of kings. *Leviathan* claims that the state is always right as long as it maintains the power to enforce the law and demand obedience.

Hobbes believed that the Leviathan should have limits, however. The state should have absolute authority to defend its people against violence, both from outside forces and from other citizens. It also had the right to pass laws to ensure peace and prosperity. But it should have no say in any other aspect of their lives. As long as the citizens do not harm one another, they should be free to act however they choose. In chapter 35 he explains this principle as "Do not that to another, which thou wouldst not have done to thyself." In other words, before you do something to someone else, think about whether you would want them to do the same thing to you.

ALLEGIANCE TO THE STATE

It is important to note that *Leviathan* does not say that monarchies are the only acceptable type of government. Hobbes himself felt that a monarchy was the best option, because the monarch could make decisions himself or herself rather than having to win the approval of a committee. But if a parliamentary government or even a democracy was given the power and could maintain the peace, then that would be the appropriate state in that situation.

As Hobbes explains in *Leviathan*, as long as the state does its job of protecting the people, it must be respected and obeyed. If the state fails, however, it has to be replaced by a new state, which is also owed allegiance. Thus, when Charles I became king of England, he also became the head of the state. Every English man owed him allegiance, including the members of Parliament. By defying him, the MPs were rebelling against the legal authority of the state and committing treason. Once Charles was deposed, however, he was no longer the head of the state because he could no longer protect the people. Parliament now had the power, which made it the legitimate government. At that point, opposing Parliament became an act of treason. Hobbes had always believed this—he had championed the

The Houses of Parliament are depicted in this engraving from 1640. The two houses are the House of Commons and the House of Lords. The struggle for power between the king and Parliament was a common theme throughout Hobbes's lifetime. After the publication of *Leviathan*, many people believed that Hobbes had shifted his allegiance from the king to Parliament. He was accused of being a traitor and developed many enemies.

monarchy only because it was the existing state at the time. But Charles's advisers saw this section of *Leviathan* as Hobbes hoping to win favor with Cromwell by giving up on the monarchy.

VIEWS ON RELIGION

Unfortunately, *Leviathan* also angered many because of its views on organized religion. The Catholics and Presbyterians took offense at Hobbes's attacks on them toward the end of the book. Other Christians found some of his earlier ideas offensive. Hobbes claimed that people were rational and behaved morally only because being moral was rational within a society. This claim meant that people had come up with their own moral codes. Traditionally, God is considered the great lawgiver, and most Christians at that time believed that God had presented man with the moral code. *Leviathan* claims otherwise. It reduces God's authority by saying that man had created his own codes without any outside help.

Christians also disapproved of Hobbes's belief that people should "do no harm." This belief went against the Christian golden rule of "do unto others as you would have them do unto you." The two sound the same at first, but the Christian rule actively encourages people to affect others. Hobbes discouraged it, because he believed that people shouldn't be required to try to improve other people's lives. They should be restricted, however, from hurting other people.

UNION OF CHURCH AND STATE

Hobbes also believed that the state had to be a true Leviathan, an all-powerful beast. That meant that it needed to have power to stop violence from every direction and could not yield power to another entity. Thus, the church and the Crown had to be

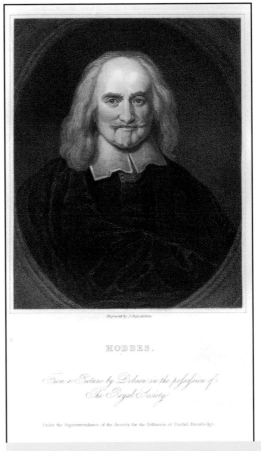

HOBBES.

From a Picture by Dobson in the possession of The Royal Society

Under the Superintendance of the Society for the Diffusion of Useful Knowledge.

The writing beneath this engraving of Hobbes reads, "From a Picture by Dobson in the possession of the Royal Society." Founded in 1660, the Royal Society is England's most prestigious science organization.

one and the same in England. This made the Church of England happy, since it supported the idea that Charles I was the head of the church as well as the lawful king. However, the idea of a united Crown and

Church of England did not go over well with people outside of the Church of England. Many Catholics, who considered the pope their supreme leader, worried that this union would further decrease the influence of the pope in England. Protestant groups such as the Presbyterians disliked the idea for a similar reason. An all-powerful Leviathan would have too much power. They feared they might lose the freedom to practice their religion.

Although *Leviathan* is a philosophical work, it does not deal in abstracts. Hobbes was utterly materialistic in his view of the world. He believed that we cannot know what exists beyond the senses. Because of this, we have to base our beliefs upon whatever our senses tell us.

Hobbes felt that everything could be explained through the movement of physical objects. The senses and reason were all that were necessary. Using your senses, you can see and feel objects and watch their movement. Using reason, you can determine their paths and move accordingly. All of life can be reduced to watching, assessing, and reacting. This can be applied to social interactions as easily as it can apply to rolling two balls toward one another. In other words, you deal with other people by studying them, seeing what they are doing, and then adjusting your plans to match, oppose, or avoid their activities.

OTHER WORKS

Hobbes is best known for five books: *Leviathan*, *Elements of Law*, and the trilogy *On the Citizen*, *On the Body*, and *On Man*. But he wrote several other books as well. His first book was a translation from Greek to Latin of Thucydides's *History of the Peloponnesian Wars*. Next was *A Short Treatise on First Principles*, a short work about mathematics and physical sensation. He wrote *Tractatus Opticus*, a short tract on optics, while in Paris in the 1640s. He then published a set of objections to his friend Descartes' *Meditations on First Philosophy*.

THE DEBATE WITH JOHN WALLIS

Hobbes was a powerful debater. He wrote several texts to attack opponents or to defend himself against their attacks. In 1656, he published *Six Lessons to the Professors of Mathematics in the University of Oxford*. This was a reply to attacks against his mathematics by people such as John Wallis, one of the most respected mathematicians in England. Part of Hobbes's problem, according to Wallis, was that he had no interest in math beyond geometry. He argued that Hobbes had not bothered to learn the math at the foundation of geometry.

THOMÆ HOBBES

Malmesburiensis

OPERA

PHILOSOPHICA,

Quæ Latinè scripsit,

OMNIA.

Antè quidem per partes, nunc autem, post cognitas omnium
Objectiones, conjunctim & accuratiùs Edita.

*Thomas Ripoll Mr Gtis Ordis Præd. pro Bibliotheca sui convø
Ontus Sta Cathæ Vr es   Mr Barchinang*

INDEFESSVS AGENDO

AMSTELODAMI,

Apud IOANNEM BLAEV,

MDCLXVIII.

Because of this, Hobbes's basic principles were utterly flawed. Hobbes responded with his *Six Lessons*. This didn't satisfy Wallis, however. He responded that he still thought Hobbes's math was flawed. Hobbes responded with *Marks of the Absurd Geometry, Rural Language, Scottish Church Politics, and Barbarisms of John Wallis, Professor of Geometry and Doctor of Divinity*. Then, Wallis countered in 1657 with *The Undoing of Mr. Hobbes's Points* (Hobbiani Puncti Dispunctio). Hobbes didn't reply to that one, and for several years the two men left each other alone.

In the spring of 1660, Hobbes fought Wallis again with a series of six dialogues about mathematical analysis. Wallis attacked Hobbes's politics next, accusing him of betraying Charles I and supporting Cromwell in *Leviathan*. Hobbes replied with *Mr. Hobbes Considered in His Loyalty, Religion, Reputation, and Manners*, which he published in 1662. This biographical letter was so effectively written that Wallis

This is the title page from Hobbes's *Opera Philosophica*. The book was one of Hobbes's later works. The edition seen here was published in 1668 in Amsterdam. Although it wasn't his most popular book, *Opera Philosophica* expands on many of the important ideas that Hobbes introduced in his earlier books.

gave up attacking Hobbes's politics. He realized that he was no match for Hobbes's political savvy.

HOBBES'S POETRY

In 1652, Hobbes wrote several poems, including one in Latin about how the clergy kept trying to steal away the power of the state. This particular poem was more than 500 verses long. It was never published, but Hobbes showed it to friends.

THE DEBATE WITH BISHOP BRAMHALL

In 1654, Bishop John Bramhall published a small treatise called *Of Liberty and Necessity*, which he addressed to Hobbes. The two men had debated religion before, and Hobbes replied privately. Unfortunately, one of his friends got a copy of the reply and published it without Hobbes's consent. Bramhall responded in 1655, by printing *A Defence of the True Liberty of Human Actions from Antecedent*

The title page of the 1656 edition of John Wallis's book *Arithmetica Infinitorum* (The Arithmetic of Infinitesimals) is pictured at right. Hobbes thought very little of the book, calling it a "scab of symbols."

Johannis Wallisii, ss. Th. D.

GEOMETRIÆ PROFESSORIS

SAVILIANI in Celeberrimà

Academia OXONIENSI,

ARITHMETICA INFINITORVM,

SIVE

Nova Methodus Inquirendi in Curvili-
neorum Quadraturam, àliaq; difficiliora
Matheseos Problemata.

OXONII,
Typis LEON: LICHFIELD Academiæ Typographi,
Impensis THO. ROBINSON. Anno 1656.

Title page of the *Arithmetica infinitorum* 1656

or Extrinsic Necessity, which contained all of his correspondence with Hobbes. Hobbes, in turn, replied in 1656 with *Questions Concerning Liberty, Necessity and Chance.* This is considered one of the first texts to specifically explain determinism, the belief that man does not have free will to choose his own fate.

Toward the end of his life, Hobbes began to indulge his old love of the classics again. In 1672, he wrote an autobiography in Latin verse. He translated the first four books of the *Odyssey* into English rhyme in 1673. In 1675, he translated the entire *Iliad* and *Odyssey*.

THE FINAL DEBATES

Although Wallis had given up attacking Hobbes's personal life and politics, the two men still argued passionately about mathematics. In 1666, Hobbes published *The Principles and Theories of Geometry* (De Principiis et Ratiocinatione Geometrarum), which attacked several professors of geometry by showing the flaws in their theories. Three years later, Hobbes presented his own solutions to several key problems in *The Squaring of the Circle, the Cubing of the Sphere, the Doubling of the Cube* (Quadratura Circuli, Cubatio Sphaerae, Duplicitio

Cubii). Wallis promptly pointed out the errors in these solutions, and the two published letters back and forth until 1678. That was also the year that Hobbes published *Ten Questions of Physiology* (Decameron Physiologicum).

In 1679, shortly before he died, *Behemoth* was published. This controversial history studied the causes of the English civil wars. Hobbes had finished the book in 1668, more than a decade earlier, but Charles II had refused to let him publish it, fearing that Parliament would attack the old man again.

THE IMPACT OF HOBBES

Great men stand by their morals and their beliefs even when the rest of the world turns against them. Hobbes often called himself a cowardly man who spent his whole life running away, yet he never backed down from an argument when he thought he was right. He risked his life many times to write about what he believed was important.

CHAPTER 6

ON THE OUTSIDE

Although he was born into the middle class, Hobbes spent most of his life with the landed gentry and the nobility. He was a tutor and personal friend to several earls, at least one lord, and one king. This earned him some acceptance in those upper social circles, but his lack of personal fortune prevented him from being truly accepted there. At the same

Thomas Hobbes passed away on December 4, 1679. He lived to be ninety-one years old, which is an amazing feat today, let alone in the seventeenth century. Although his age is beginning to show in the portrait above, old age didn't hinder Hobbes's love of writing and philosophy. Hobbes translated the works of the ancient Greek poet Homer when he was in his eighties and published his last book, *Behemoth*, in the same year he died.

time, education, manners, and interests prevented him from being accepted by the working class or even most of the merchant class. In many ways, Hobbes was a man on the outside looking in.

Hobbes was also a Christian, but for most of his life he was hated by at least one Christian sect. The Puritans and Catholics disliked him because he had supported the king's position as the head of the Church of England. The Protestants did not trust him, including the followers of the Church of England who thought he had turned traitor and given support to Cromwell. Above all, Christians of all denominations despised him for his beliefs that went again their traditions. Especially disliked were his claims that moral codes were not written by God and his belief that the Christian ideal of doing good works may not be necessary to create a peaceful society.

THE MANY SIDES OF HOBBES

Part of his difficulties in gaining acceptance lay in the fact that Hobbes kept changing careers and interests. He had been an able scholar and tutor, and his interest in the classics and in translation supported that occupation. But then he discovered mathematics and seemed to forget about the classics for many years. Then he learned philosophy and set aside most of his geometry for social theory. Years later, Hobbes went back to geometry, but by then he was known primarily as a writer and philosopher.

Hobbes's problems as a mathematician did not help his fame or his popularity either. When he first began studying the subject, many people believed he was one of the finest mathematicians of the age. But Wallis and others pointed out that Hobbes's knowledge of math was limited and flawed. Rather than expand his knowledge and master the other areas of math, Hobbes continued to concentrate on geometry alone. He defended his theories as passionately as ever, even when they had been proven wrong by far more experienced mathematicians. His refusal to acknowledge his mistakes made him many additional enemies.

UNPOPULAR OPINIONS

The biggest reason for anyone to dislike Hobbes was his social theories. At a time when most of England was protesting against the king, Hobbes wrote book after book stating that the king must always be obeyed. Hobbes believed that whatever the king did was right and just, solely because he was the head of the state and the state could not be wrong or unjust. He never claimed that the king would always be the wisest man or make the best decisions. That wasn't

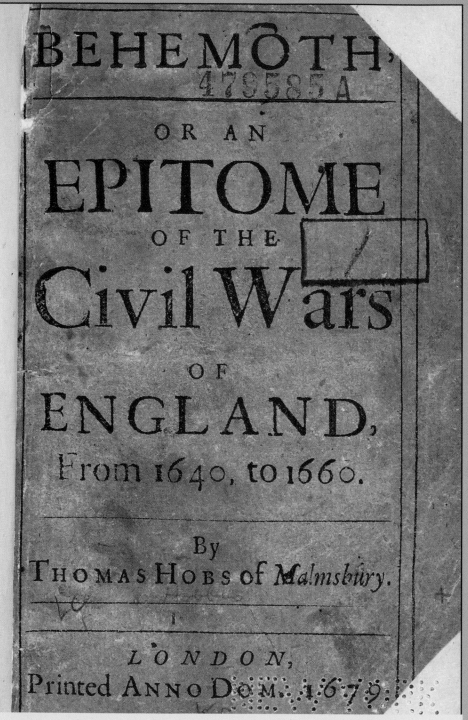

BEHEMOTH,

OR AN

EPITOME

OF THE

Civil Wars

OF

ENGLAND,

From 1640, to 1660.

By

THOMAS HOBS of *Malmsbury*.

LONDON,
Printed ANNO DOM. 1679.

As can be seen in the title page of this 1679 edition of *Behemoth*, Hobbes's last name was also spelled "Hobs," and the town of Malmesbury was spelled "Malmsbury." In the seventeenth century, people were more concerned about pronouncing words correctly than in spelling them correctly. In these two examples, regardless of how the words are spelled, they are pronounced the same.

what his countrymen wanted to hear. Only Royalists supported Hobbes's theories because his view agreed with their own. Or so they thought. As Hobbes revealed later, however, he was not loyal to the king himself. Instead, Hobbes was loyal to the state, in whatever form it took at the time. So when Charles I was killed and Cromwell took his place, Hobbes was loyal to Cromwell, the new head of state. Most people could not understand how Hobbes was still loyal to his principles and to the nation as a whole. All they saw was that he had switched from following the king to supporting Cromwell and that made him a traitor.

Because Hobbes spoke out for what he believed in, he had many enemies. He moved back and forth between England and continental Europe for most of his life to avoid attacks from those who felt insulted by his books. Even after Charles II came to power and brought Hobbes to his court, many courtiers and politicians took great pleasure in attacking Hobbes.

By the end of his life, however, Hobbes had earned the respect of almost everyone in England. More and more people began reading his books. They finally understood what he meant about the state and why he had seemed to switch his loyalties over the years. They understood his theories and admired the clarity of his thought. This must have made Hobbes feel that all his years of hard work had been justified.

BELATED RESPECT

Today, Hobbes is remembered as one of the great thinkers of the seventeenth century. He is often considered a founder of modern political philosophy and one of the fathers of political liberalism. The concept of the social contract is probably his best-known and most influential idea. Many great thinkers would build upon this idea in their own work, including people such as John Stuart Mill, Edmund Burke, and Thomas Paine.

Hobbes had an enormous impact on British political, social, and economic theory. Jeremy Bentham borrowed his principle of hedonism (that people are interested in personal gratification of the senses). Adam Smith and other economists took up Hobbes's belief that society is a matter of finding a balance between contradictory self-interests. Both David Hume and Friedrich von Hayek borrowed his theory about the evolution of morality and law.

Of course, Hobbes had predecessors of his own. A century before him, Niccolò Machiavelli had revealed the harsh realities of politics, showing just what the leader of a nation needed to do in order to govern effectively. In many ways, Machiavelli was the first modern political thinker. He was willing to

HOBBES AND THE ENLIGHTENMENT

In many ways, Hobbes is the perfect example of an Enlightenment thinker. He believed that logic and reason could find answers to social problems. He felt that science, not religion, held the key to a strong society. He believed that social structures should be kept only if they worked and should be removed and replaced if they failed the people. He believed that society must work for the masses, providing the best result for the largest number of people.

However, according to some historians, Hobbes didn't live during the Enlightenment. They argue that Hobbes lived in the period just before the Enlightenment. Regardless, it cannot be denied that Hobbes was one of the first men to apply scientific reasoning to human interactions. His books, especially *Leviathan*, were radical in their suggestions. The people who read them were fascinated by Hobbes's ideas and by his approach to the world and its ills. Even if he was not technically part of the period known as the Enlightenment, his writings and his thoughts influenced the men who would later lead that movement.

talk about the ugly truths of political power because he saw politics as an activity that had no ties to religious faith. Unlike Hobbes, Machiavelli offered only practical suggestions with no underlying theory to explain it. Hobbes followed Machiavelli by talking about politics in nonreligious terms, but Hobbes provided an entire philosophy to support his specific statements. He gave us a belief system to build upon. Because of this, Hobbes's theories are arguably more versatile than those of Machiavelli and more relevant today.

LOCKE ANSWERS HOBBES

John Locke appeared a few years after Hobbes and is often considered Hobbes's philosophical opposite. Locke tried to answer many of the questions Hobbes had presented. How can humans peacefully live

This portrait of Niccoló Machiavelli (1469–1527) was painted in 1600 by Santi di Tito. Despite being from different countries and separated by a hundred years of history, Machiavelli and Hobbes shared a number of things in common. Most notably, both liked to write about how politics and government worked. Both were also pessimistic about human nature, believing that people were apt to cheat, lie, and steal when there was a competition for power.

together? What happens when the old explanations for the state's authority are no longer sufficient? How much power should the state have? And what, if anything, can stop the state from taking control of every aspect of our lives?

Locke felt that the state needed more limits in order to protect the rights of the citizens. He also felt that Hobbes was too willing to accept a ruler and to condone that ruler's actions. For Locke, a person's natural state is not automatically chaos, and the king is not always right just because he is the king. Most people today side with Locke and his understanding of human nature and politics. However, this doesn't negate the contribution of Hobbes. Locke's arguments could not have existed without Hobbes's framework.

Today, Hobbes has won respect for the way he structured his thoughts. He approached all of his work systematically and logically, using mathematical principles to examine human nature and activity. He studied language and the way that words were used in order to use them as effectively as possible. Even people who have laughed at his math have admired the careful way he approached each problem. He looked at humanity and society the same way—using only the principles of logic and science. Because of this, Hobbes is considered one of the first social scientists.

A MAN OF HIS TIMES

Hobbes was very much the product of his time and his studies. His education in the classics showed him that history was an important tool for understanding the present. Living through a tumultuous period in English history allowed Hobbes to see firsthand how politics affected everyone in the nation.

The political philosophy of John Locke (1632–1704) greatly influenced the writers of the U.S. Constitution and the Declaration of Independence. Locke also wrote about psychology. He is best known for his book *An Essay Concerning Human Understanding* (1690), which details his theory about how people learn.

When he discovered the beauty of geometry, with its clean lines and clear relationships, Hobbes saw a way to simplify society. He hoped that by explaining society in mathematical terms he could show everyone how to set aside their differences. That was the goal behind books such as *Elements of Law* and *Leviathan*.

Hobbes knew that most people only wanted peace and security. One of his goals was to show

95

them how to get it. He talked about the role of the state and its citizens because he wanted to prove that politics was not as complicated as it seemed. The social contract was very simple, and if everyone agreed to it, they would find themselves living in a more peaceful society.

A FRAMEWORK FOR SOCIETY

Hobbes's theories provide a solid framework, even today, for many societies. They show exactly what people can expect from their rulers and what their rulers owe them in return. Hobbes presents a model for the ideal society, where everyone exists peacefully and feels secure. At the same time, there is enough freedom for individual happiness. Hobbes's model is based upon human interactions and upon the idea that we are always in motion. His model is built to adjust to new conditions. It is a constantly evolving form, designed to grow with us and to suit our current needs. This is the legacy Thomas Hobbes left us. He described a way to live with others without war or violence, governed by logic and rules designed to keep us safe from harm.

TIMELINE

1588	Thomas Hobbes is born on April 5, in Malmesbury, England.
1592	Hobbes begins his education.
1595	Hobbes's father, Thomas Hobbes, flees to London, abandoning his family.
1603	Hobbes enters Magdalen Hall, at the University of Oxford.
1608	Hobbes graduates from Oxford and begins to tutor young William Cavendish.
1610	Hobbes takes his first trip to continental Europe.
1625	Charles I becomes king of England after the death of James I.
1628	Hobbes discovers geometry.
1629	Hobbes becomes the tutor for the son of Sir Gervase Clifton. He takes a second trip to continental Europe.
1631	Hobbes returns to England to tutor the son of William Cavendish.
1634	Hobbes takes a third trip to continental Europe. Hobbes meets Marin Mersenne, Galilei Galileo, René Descartes, and others. Hobbes develops his theories on geometry and society.
1637	Charles I tries to force Scotland to use the Church of England prayer book. When the Scots refuse, Charles raises an army to attack them.
1640	Hobbes circulates his manuscript *Elements of Law*. Charles I dissolves Parliament in May. In November, Hobbes flees to Paris.
1642	*On the Citizen* is published. Parliamentary forces battle the army of Charles I at Edgehill.
1646	Hobbes tutors the future Charles II in mathematics.

1647	Hobbes suffers a severe illness but recovers. He publishes the second edition of *On the Citizen*.
1649	Charles I is executed. Oliver Cromwell takes over as ruler of England.
1650	*Elements of Law* is published without Hobbes's consent.
1651	*Leviathan* is published. Hobbes returns to England.
1655	*On the Body* is published.
1658	*On Man* is published.
1660	The English monarchy is restored when Charles II assumes the throne.
1666	The Great Fire of London. Parliament considers trying Hobbes for heresy.
1668	Hobbes finishes *Behemoth*.
1672	Hobbes writes his autobiography.
1675	Hobbes publishes translations of the *Iliad* and the *Odyssey*.
1679	*Behemoth* is published. Thomas Hobbes dies on December 4.

GLOSSARY

abstract Vague and undefined. "Love" and "hate" are abstract ideas. They cannot be touched or seen or even described precisely.

amnesty A pardon granted by the government for one's crimes.

anarchy A state of society in which there is no government.

Anglicanism Relating to England or its people. Also, relating to the Anglican Church, the official Church of England.

appendix Additional material found at the end of a book.

atheism Not believing in any religion, or in the existence of a god or gods.

classics The study of ancient art and culture, particularly Greece and Rome.

clergy Ministers or priests in a Christian church.

courtier Member of the king or queen's inner circle of friends and advisers.

deductive reasoning The process of thinking through a problem by first considering what you know and then using that to reach a conclusion. The opposite is inductive reasoning, where you determine the conclusion first and then figure out what led to that result.

depose Removing someone from a position of power.

dialogue A conversation between two or more people; a piece of writing consisting of a conversation between two or more people.

fallible Capable of making a mistake.

gentry The class of wealthy men who owned land but did not have titles of nobility.

hawking The sport of hunting with hawks, also known as falconry.

heresy Religious views that do not agree with the dominant religious views. The person who has these views is known as a heretic.

House of Commons One half of the British parliament. Members of the House of Commons are elected to their seat by the people in their district. The other half of the British parliament is the House of Lords.

liberalism Political beliefs that favor progress and reform.

logical reasoning Thinking in a clear and logical fashion. This involves starting with known facts, and then determining everything from those facts.

lord A wealthy landowner in English society, often with ties to the king or queen.

materialistic Focused upon physical objects and activities.

monarchy A form of government ruled by a king or a queen.

moral code Set of beliefs or values.

optics The study of vision and lenses.

parliament A government assembly in which people meet to discuss matters of government and to decide what the government should do.

pension Money paid out to someone who has retired. Usually it is paid by his or her former employer.

Puritan A member of a group of Protestants who felt that the Catholic Church had become corrupt and needed to be purified.

rational Requiring the use of the mind; intellectual.

Royalist Someone who supports the king or queen.

social construct Something created by society that does not exist beyond society. For example, a speed limit is a social construct, because if you lived on an island by yourself, you would not need to worry about how fast you were driving.

squaring a circle Constructing a square with the same area as a circle.

treason Attempt to overthrow the legal government or its rulers.

treatise A scholarly article, often outlining the solution to some problem or explaining a topic.

tyranny A form of government in which the ruler has absolute power and dominates the people of his or her country through fear and intimidation.

verse A line of words arranged in a rhythmic pattern, as is done in poetry.

vicar An Anglican parish priest.

FOR MORE INFORMATION

Center for Seventeenth- and
  Eighteenth-Century Studies
310 Royce Hall
UCLA
Los Angeles, CA 90095-1404
(310) 206-8552
Web site: http://www.humnet.ucla.edu/
  humnet/c1718cs

Thomas Hobbes Society
14 Monks Park
Milbourne, Malmesbury SN16 9JF
England
016 6682 6051

WEB SITES

Due to the changing nature of Internet
links, the Rosen Publishing Group, Inc.,
has developed an online list of Web
sites related to the subject of this
book. This site is updated regularly.
Please use this link to access the list:

http://www.rosenlinks.com/phen/thho

FOR FURTHER READING

Baigrie, Brian S., ed. *The Renaissance and the Scientific Revolution: Biographical Portraits.* New York, NY: Scribner, 2001.

Davis, Kenneth C. *Don't Know Much About the Kings and Queens of England.* New York, NY: Harper Collins, 2002.

Dunn, John. *The Enlightenment.* San Diego, CA: Lucent Books, 1999.

Gerdes, Louise I. *The 1600s: Headlines in History.* San Diego, CA: Greenhaven Press, 2001.

Greenblatt, Miriam. *Elizabeth I and Tudor England.* New York, NY: Benchmark, 2002.

Lace, William W. *Oliver Cromwell and the English Civil War in World History.* Berkeley Heights, NJ: Enslow, 2003.

Law, Stephen. *Philosophy Rocks!* New York, NY: Volo, 2002.

Magee, Bryan. *The Great Philosophers: An Introduction to Western Philosophy.* New York, NY: Oxford University Press, 2000.

Shields, Charles J. *The Great Plague and Fire of London*. Philadelphia, PA: Chelsea House, 2002.

Smith, David L. *Oliver Cromwell: Politics and Religion in the English Revolution 1640–1658*. New York, NY: Cambridge University Press, 1991.

Weate, Jeremy. *A Young Person's Guide to Philosophy*. New York, NY: DK Publishing, 1998.

BIBLIOGRAPHY

Aubrey, John. *Brief Lives*. Richard Barber, ed. Woodbridge, England: Boydell Press, 2004.

Fonseca, Gonçalo L., and Leanne J. Ussher. "Thomas Hobbes, 1588–1679." Retrieved August 1, 2004 (http://cepa.newschool. edu/het/profiles/hobbes.htm).

Hobbes, Thomas. *Leviathan*. Edwin Curley, ed. Indianapolis, IN: Hackett, 1994.

Hobbes, Thomas. *On the Citizen*. Richard Tuck and Michael Silverthorne, eds. Cambridge, MA: Cambridge University Press, 1998.

Martinich, Aloysius P. *Thomas Hobbes*. New York, NY: St. Martin's Press, 1997.

Molesworth, Sir William, ed. *The English Works of Thomas Hobbes*. Oxford, England: Oxford University Press, 1962.

O'Connor, J. J., and E. F. Robertson. "Thomas Hobbes." Retrieved August 29, 2004 (http://www-groups.dcs. st-and.ac.uk/~history/Mathematicians/ Hobbes.html).

"The Philosophy of Thomas Hobbes." The Radical Academy. Retrieved September 8, 2004 (http://www.radicalacademy.com/philfthomashobbes.htm).

Sarkissian, Robert. "Thomas Hobbes." Retrieved July 12, 2004 (http://www.island-of-freedom.com/hobbes.htm).

Sorrell, Tom, ed. *The Cambridge Companion to Hobbes.* Cambridge, MA: Cambridge University Press, 1989.

Sorrell, Tom. *Hobbes.* London, England: Routledge, 1996.

"Thomas Hobbes." Retrieved September 2, 2004 (http://en.wikipedia.org/wiki/Thomas_Hobbes).

"Thomas Hobbes." Biography.com. Retrieved August 23, 2004 (http://www.biography.com/search/article.jsp?aid=9340461).

Tuck, Richard. *Hobbes.* Oxford, England: Oxford University Press, 1989.

Williams, Garrath. "Thomas Hobbes: Moral and Political Philosophy." The Internet Encyclopedia of Philosophy. Retrieved September 10, 2004 (http://www.utm.edu/research/iep/h/hobmoral.htm).

Index

About the Author

Like Hobbes, Aaron Rosenberg studied the classics—he has two degrees in English, including one in English literature. He also followed Hobbes's path of tutoring and writing—Mr. Rosenberg has taught college-level English for several years and has written nonfiction books on a variety of subjects. Currently, he lives in New York City.

Credits

Cover, pp. 50–51 akg-images/British Library; Cover (inset), pp.3, 8 Burghley House Collection, Lincolnshire, UK/Bridgeman Art Library; p. 6 Map p. 545 from CIVILIZATION PAST & PRESENT, 10th ed. by Palmira Brummett et al. Copyright © 2003 by Addison-Wesley Educational Publishers, Inc. Reprinted by permission of Pearson Education, Inc.; p.13 Erich Lessing/Art Resource, NY; pp. 16, 58, 78 © Archivo Iconografico, S.A./Corbis; pp. 18, 37, 67, 73 Private Collection/Bridgeman Art Library; p. 21 Collection of the Earl of Pembroke, Wilton House, Wilts., UK/Bridgeman Art Library; p. 24 Ackermann and Johnson Ltd., London, UK/Bridgeman Art Library; pp. 26–27 © Sotheby's/akg-images; p. 28 John Bethell/Bridgeman Art Library; p. 31 © Gianni Dagli Orti/Corbis; p. 32 Roy Miles Fine Paintings/Bridgeman Art Library; p. 36 Musee de la Ville de Paris, Musee Carnavalet, Paris, France/Bridgeman Art Library; p. 41 Giraudon/Art Resource, NY; p. 42 Cheltenham Art Gallery & Museums, Gloucestershire, UK/Bridgeman Art Library; p. 45 Leeds Museums and Galleries (City Art Gallery) UK/Bridgeman Art Library; p. 48 Fitzwilliam Museum, University of Cambridge, UK/Bridgeman Art Library; pp. 52, 95 Philip Mould, Historical Portraits Ltd, London, UK/Bridgeman Art Library; p. 54 Mary Evans Picture Library; p. 64 National Portrait Gallery, London; p. 75 © Michael Nicholson/Corbis; p. 81 Science, Industry & Business Library, The New York Public Library, Astor, Lenox and Tilden Foundations; p. 85 © Bettmann/Corbis; p. 88 General Research Division, The New York Public Library, Astor, Lenox and Tilden Foundations; p. 93 akg-images/Electa.

Designer: Evelyn Horovicz
Editor: Brian Belval
Photo Researcher: Sherri Liberman